For Louise Bolongaro – J.W.

For Yoko and Yoko, with love from Rosie

Clarion Books
a Houghton Mifflin Company imprint
215 Park Avenue South, New York, NY 10003
Text copyright © 2006 by Jeanne Willis
Illustrations copyright © 2006 by Rosie Reeve
First published in Great Britain in 2006 by Puffin Books.
First American edition, 2007.
The illustrations were executed in ink, colored pencil, and collage.
All rights reserved.

For information about permission to reproduce selections from
this book, write to Permissions, Houghton Mifflin Company,
215 Park Avenue South, New York, NY 10003.

www.houghtonmifflinbooks.com
Printed in China.

*Full cataloging information is available from
the Library of Congress.*

LC#: 2006006242
ISBN-10: 0-618-78195-1
ISBN-13: 978-0-618-78195-9
EAN: 9780618781959

10 9 8 7 6 5 4 3 2 1

# Delilah D.
## at the Library

by
**Jeanne Willis**

Illustrated by
**Rosie Reeve**

CLARION BOOKS

*New York*

My name is Queen Delilah D.

I come from a land far, far away.

But my mother likes to keep it a secret.

She always says,

"But Delilah, darling, you were born here!"
And,

"No, Delilah.
You cannot wear a crown to school.
You are not
the
Queen."

That's just nonsense.
If you don't believe me,
   ask my brother, Smallboy.
      But you won't understand the answer
because Smallboy speaks only
                    Faraway Language.

And don't ask Daddy,
   because he's busy.

This is Gigi, my new sitter.
She is supposed to look after me and Smallboy
until Mother comes home.
She comes from a different faraway land
called France.

Gigi says,
"Come, Delilah, my little cabbage.
Let us go to the library."

Oh, good.
I love looking at books.

And smelling them.

And shutting them like this . . .

SNAP!

when I get
to the end.

The library is full of extremely interesting books:
some have **pictures**,
some have **words**
and this one
has a squashed
**baked bean**
on
page 5.

But do you know? Things are different
in my Faraway Land.
Where I come from,
they always give you
**free**
cupcakes
at the library.

Smallboy is hungry, so I ask Gigi,
   "When will they bring the cupcakes?"
And she says,
   "What is cupscake?
I am not understanding.
      Ask that Library Anne."

So me and Smallboy go
      and ask Library Anne,
but she says,
   "No food in here, please!"

And I say,

"Really?? Where I come from, everyone eats in the library. A man walks around with a big tray, and he shouts,

'WHO WANTS CUPCAKES? WHO WANTS DOUGHNUTS?'"

"Shhh!" says Library Anne.
But everybody says, "Ooh, are there cupcakes?
Are they free? We want doughnuts!"

"Now, that," says Library Anne,
"is why we don't shout in the library."

"I don't know where **you** come from, young lady, but we have **different** rules in this library."

I tell her I come from a land far, far away.

"Well, **run along** and find a nice **book** about it," she says.

So I run along, but Library Anne calls,
"No running in
the library, please!"

Which is odd, because where I come from,
everyone runs in the library.

Anyway, I try to find
a book about the land
where I come from,
but I can't.

Anyone would think
there's no such place.

Then Smallboy says, in Faraway Language,
"Try up there!"
So I start
to climb,

but Library Anne says,
"My goodness, come down!
That is not how we fetch
a book!"

I say,

"Oh, I'm sorry, but I couldn't find the trapeze. Where I come from, there is a trapeze to reach the too-high books."

"Hey, I like the trapeze idea,"
says Mrs. Woolly Hat. "I'm short.
I never get to read the
too-high books."

Library Anne says,
"There are much more sensible
ways of reaching books."

"I will **help** you
find the book
**properly.**"

"Now," she says,
"tell me the **name** of
the **land** where you come from."

But I **can't**, because
it's **very** hard to say.

Smallboy tells her in Faraway Language,
but she doesn't understand.

So I explain that we come from

a tiny little island between

Jafrica

and

Smindia.

But Library Anne has **never heard** of those places.

Library Anne opens a **big** book and says,
"Here is a **map** of the **world**.
Can you **point** to
where you come from?"

Would you **believe** it?
The person who drew the map
**forgot** to put it on.

Here it is—
a map of the land where I come from.
You can't read its name because it's under my drawing of a
Jafrican smelliphant, which is
kind
of
like
a
Smindian
oliphant,
only
smellier.

the caves

the camp

the beach

So I give Library Anne
a map **I made** to show her
what the world is **really** like.

Where I come from, we have our own animals,
our own **rules**, our own **everything**.
We **even** have our own **song**, called
"HOORAY FOR QUEEN DELILAH."
"I'd love to hear it!" says Mrs. Woolly Hat.

So I stand on a chair and sing it.
Mrs. Woolly Hat joins in.

It goes like this:

Hooray for Queen Delilah,
So beautiful, so brave.
Hurrah for Queen Delilah,
The Kingdom she will save.
Oh, shout Hoorah! Oh, shout Hooray!
Shout out loud and strong.
Hooray for Queen Delilah D.,
Who wrote this lovely song!
Tra-la!

Library Anne says,
"I wish I lived far, far away.
Please stop singing!"

Then she says,
"Would you like to
**borrow** a **book**
before you **leave?**"

Where I come from,
we **don't borrow** books
and **leave!**

We all **bring**

our blankets and toys, and a beautiful princess reads to us until we fall asleep.

"Cupcakes! Blankets! Toys!
That's how to run a library,"
says everyone.

"There are days," says Library Anne,
"when I wish I was
an astronaut."

"Delilah,
    darling,"
says Gigi.

"I think it is time
    to say 'Au Revoir.'"

Where she comes from,
that means Goodbye.

We go home.
I tell my mother about the library.
It was **extremely** fun.
And I borrowed a lovely book
called TROPICAL DISEASES.

But it was **nothing like** the library
in the **land** where I come from.

"But Delilah, darling," she says,
"you come from here! We all do."

We don't, though.
She's just pretending.
Silly old thing.

TROPICAL
DISEASES

TROPICAL DISEASES

"Oh, Mommy," I sigh,
"sometimes I think you're living
in a world of your own."

Yes, I know I'm holding my
library book **upside down.**
Where **I** come from,
that's how **everybody** reads.